Penny Loves

PiNK

For Charli

Penny Loves

PiNK

Cori Doerrfeld

SCHOLASTIC INC.
New York Toronto London Auckland
Sydney Mexico City New Delhi Hong Kong

My name is Penny, and I love PINK!

I love my pink shirts . . .

. . . my pink shoes . . .

. . . and my sparkly pink sunglasses.

I love my pink parties . . .

. . . and I love my pink potty, too.

I love pink cotton candy . . .

. . . pink ice cream . . .

. . . and riding my pink bike
past pink flowers.

I love everything pink!

I think I'd even love a pink monster!

"Penny! Come meet your new baby brother!"

I don't like blue. I only love . . .

. . . . **pink!**

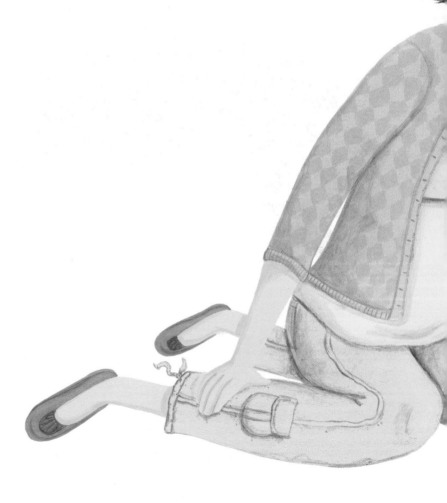

And I love YOU, Parker!

Even more than I love pink!

Penny Loves
PARKER!